Wolf and Dog

WOLF AND DOG

Sylvia Vanden Heede

Illustrated by Marije Tolman

Translated by Bill Nagelkerke

GECKO PRESS

BACON

Dog is Wolf's cousin.
Wolf is Dog's cousin.
That's strange because:

Wolf is wild.
And Dog is tame.

Wolf lives in a forest on top of a hill.
Dog doesn't.
Dog has a basket.
And a boss.

Dog is white with a patch around one eye.
Wolf doesn't have a patch.
He's gray from head to tail.

Wolf rings Dog's doorbell.
There's a notice on the door:

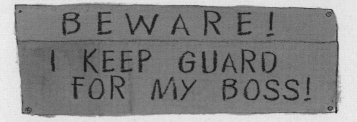

The boss isn't home.
That's just as well.
Wolf is scared of Dog's boss.

"Hello Dog," growls Wolf.

"Hello Wolf," barks Dog.
"Don't bite me, will you?
After all, we're cousins.

I know that.
But I know you, too.
You're still a wolf.
You bite when you're hungry."

Wolf snaps his mouth shut.
He looks glum.
It's true what Dog says.
When he's hungry, he bites.
He can't help it.
A wolf is always hungry.
"What have you got to eat?" asks Wolf.
He licks his chops.

"Bacon," says Dog.
"And bread. And cheese.
And some lettuce leaves."

Wolf screws up his nose.
"Rats!"
He hates lettuce!
"Lettuce is green.
And I don't eat green.
Give me red instead.
Red meat!
Raw meat!
Red and raw and bloody!
Green's for cows.
Or goats.
Or lambs or calves."

"Green is good for the waistline," says Dog.
He pats his stomach.
"Let us slim with lettuce.
Let us.
Get it?"

"Ha, ha!" laughs Wolf. "That's a good one!
But it's not true.
You eat lettuce.
You're not slim.
In fact, you're as big as a…"

"Yes, yes," says Dog quickly.
"I know you like rhymes.
But not now or I'll bark.
I'll bark like crazy.
Then my boss will come.
Is that what you want?"

Wolf goes quiet.
He watches Dog.
Dog fries bacon in a pan.
Fatty bacon!
The bacon spits: "Sizz, sizz!"
That's what it says as it sizzles in fat.

Mmm, it smells so good!
It drives Wolf nuts.
Mad with hunger.
"Nearly ready," says Dog.
He turns down the heat.
He takes out a plate.
A knife and a fork.
He puts them beside the plate.
He fetches the pan…

But what's this?
Where's the bacon?
It's gone! It's been eaten!

"Wolf!" calls Dog.
"Was that you?
Did you eat the bacon?
Straight from the pan?
In one gulp?"

"Yes," says Wolf.
He wipes his chops.
He laughs.
He's not even sorry!
"My stomach was empty.
The pan was full.
Now the pan's empty
and my stomach's full."

Dog sighs.
"Oh, Wolf," he says.
"You sure are a wild one.
You wolf down your food.
You swallow it whole!
You don't use a knife and fork.
You don't even use a plate!"

Wolf burps.
"There's not much cleaning up to do," he says.
Which is true.

ITCH

Dog has an itch.
An itch on his head.
An itch on his tail.
An itch on his belly.
An itch on his back.
He scratches with his paw.
He nips at his fur.
Nothing helps.
The itch won't leave him alone!

"I think I have a flea," says Dog.
"A flea's biting me."

"A flea?" laughs Wolf.
"Only one?
I have at least ten.
If not more."

Dog is alarmed.
"Really?" he asks.
"Yes, really," says Wolf.
"Not that I count them.
Sometimes they go away.
Sometimes they come back.
Sometimes I catch one or two.
But I never get rid of them all.
Never!
But hey, a wolf gets used to them.
There's no choice.
After a while I hardly notice."

"I do!" snaps Dog.
"An itch makes me twitch!"

"Ha ha! That rhymes," laughs Wolf.
"I love a good rhyme.
Even a flea is fun for me."

Dog doesn't laugh.
"Fleas are no fun at all!" he barks.
He scratches and scratches.
"Rats to you!"
He's so cross!
Cross with the flea.
Cross with the itch.

Suddenly Dog says:
"I know I got it from you, Wolf!"
Wolf is surprised.
"What?" he asks. "Whose?
Where from? How?
What did you get from me?"

Dog pants.
He scratches again.
"The flea," he snarls.
"It was yours, Wolf!
I got it from you.
You know I did.

The day you came to my place.
When you ate the bacon.
My bacon.
From my pan!
In my house!
When my boss wasn't there!"

"Oh," says Wolf.
"Is that right?"
He's silent for a moment.
He gives Dog a look.
A sly look.
He scowls.
And he laughs a little.
But it's not a very nice laugh.
It's a fake laugh.

"Now I get it," says Wolf.
"That's where the flea's gone.
I thought something was missing.
But what? What was it?
I didn't know.

But now I do.
It was the flea.
I didn't give it to you.
You're wrong about that.
You took it from me.
You're a thief, Dog!
You stole my flea!"

Dog turns pale.
His nose turns white.
So does the patch around his eye.
Wolf bares his teeth.
"Give me my flea," he growls.
"Hurry up!
Grab him with your teeth.
Or shall I do it?
You want me to bite you?
I'm so hungry.
I could swallow you whole.
Come here so I can get hold of you!"

Dog is scared, very scared!
Wolf is his cousin.
He knows that.
But a wolf is a wolf.
A wild animal can't be tamed.

"Watch it," Dog whimpers.
"Watch it, or I'll bark!
I'll bark as loudly as I can:

Boss! Boss!
There's a wolf in the forest!
Is that what you want?"

Wolf snaps his mouth shut.
He is quiet for a moment.
He's not growling now.
"Well, rats to you," he says.
"You keep the flea.
It's a swap.
You let me eat
that tasty treat.
In return: a flea,
to you from me."

It rhymes.
Wolf laughs.
"I love a good rhyme," he says.
And Dog laughs too.
Things have worked out well.
A flea can bite, it's true.
But not as hard as a wolf!

POISON

Wolf rings the doorbell.
"Ah, here's Dog!" he grins.
"How's my flea?
Is he eating well?
Does he bite now and then?"
"You bet," says Dog.

He scratches his ear and says:
"Your flea is fine.
But not for much longer.
See this?"
He shows Wolf the collar around his neck.

Wolf smirks.
"That's a collar," he scoffs.
"A snug neck-warmer.
It suits you, Dog.
It reminds me of a song.
I'll sing it for you:

You're a basket-and-a-boss dog,
A game-of-catch-and-toss dog.
A gentle-as-a-lamb dog,
A see-how-good-I-am dog!"

Dog doesn't like it much.
He has a quick think.
"I know a song, too," he says. "Listen."

Dog barks in a husky voice:
"*A wolf's as wild and wicked as a wolf will be.*"

Wolf tilts his head back.
"Hmm, not bad," he says.
The words go well together.
They're nice and short.
The trouble is,
you can't hold a note.
And you sing out of tune."

"I started before I was quite ready," says Dog.
He takes a deep breath.

"I may be tame but I'll get that bug.
This killer-collar isn't snug.
Because of it,
The flea won't be."

"Ha, ha!" Wolf laughs out loud.
"What a strange song!
Just listen to what you said:
The flea won't be.
That makes no sense.
What won't the flea be?"

"I know it's hard to follow," says Dog.
"But 'be' rhymes nicely with 'flea'. "

"It's a silly rhyme," Wolf says.

Dog growls.
He is very out of sorts now.
"Be quiet, Wolf," he says.
"I'm going to sing my song once more.
Without 'be'.
It's possible.
Just listen!"

And Dog sings:

"A wolf's as wild and wicked as a wolf will be.
I may be tame but I'll get that bug.
This killer-collar isn't snug.
It won't kill me.
It'll kill the flea."

That gives Wolf a real shock.
"Kill!" he cries.
"Did I hear that right?
Did you say 'kill'?"

"Yes, Wolf," Dog sighs.
"It will kill the flea.
Don't look so sad.
It can't be helped.
Blame my boss.
He doesn't want fleas in the house.
He put this flea collar round my neck.
There's poison in the collar, you see.
It doesn't do me any harm.
But it harms the flea.
Ah, it's terrible.
In a little while the flea won't be!"

Dog brushes away a tear.
He blows his nose.
He gives a deep, deep sigh.
He looks very sad.

But suddenly he smiles.
He says:
"I know what we can do, Wolf.
You're wild.

You have no boss.
You have no collar.
Isn't that so?"

"That's so." Wolf nods proudly.
"I'm as wild as they come."

Dog's smile grows.
"So the flea should hop over to you," he suggests.
Wolf shakes his head.
"Oh, no," he says.
"Definitely not, Dog.
That's not going to happen."
But Dog insists.
"Give the flea a chance, Wolf.
Go on, save him while you can."

And do you know what Dog does?
He sidles up to Wolf.
The flea springs out…
And there!
He's back on Wolf.

"Rats!" cries Wolf.
"It's biting!"
Dog laughs.
"Oh, Wolf," he says.
"*A flea is wild, not tame and still.*
And just like you, he bites at will."

And that rhymes!

RATS!

The weather is nice.
The sun is shining.
There's a breeze,
but it isn't very cold.

Dog looks out the window.
"I think I'll go for a ride," he says.
"I'll put on my coat.
And wear my cap."
Dog is proud of his cap.
It's the sort that has a peak.

Look, there goes Dog.
He's whistling a tune.
The cap suits him very well.
And he looks smart in his coat.

Who's over there?
It's Wolf.
Dog stops whistling.

He takes off his cap.
He nods and bows.
He says hello.

"How do you like my cap?" he asks.
"Pack!" says Wolf.
And he laughs out loud.

"Pack?" Dog asks.
"I have no pack.
I'm not going far.
Where should I go, Wolf?
This is where I live."
"Evil!" Wolf calls out next.
And he laughs even louder.

Dog sighs.
This isn't very nice.
Wolf's making fun of him!
Dog had been enjoying himself.
Out and about in his cap and coat.

"What's the matter with you, Wolf?" says Dog.
"It was strange what you just did."
"Did," says Wolf.
"Did is did!
And did it stays.
It's true!
Try turning it around.
Then you'll see."

"Oh," says Dog.
Now he gets it.

"Cap" becomes "pack."
And "live" becomes "evil,"
But "did" stays "did,"
no matter how you twist or turn it.

Dog puts his cap back on.
He buttons up his coat.

"Isn't this a great game?" asks Wolf.
Dog shakes his head.
"No," he says.
"On!" yells Wolf.
He rolls on the ground.
He's loving this!

But Dog doesn't laugh.
To him it's a silly game.
Still, he might as well try it.
He thinks hard.
Then he says, slyly:
"Wolf, you really are a star."
"Rats!" cried Wolf.

And he's absolutely right.

FAMILY TREE

Dog goes to visit Wolf.
He takes a book with him.
The book belongs to the boss.

"Hello Dog," says Wolf.
"Hello Wolf," says Dog.
"Don't bite me.
You're my cousin, remember.
But you're still a wolf.
And you might bite,
even though I've brought a book."

Wolf snaps his mouth shut.
"A book?" he asks.
"Why would I want a book?
I don't read."
Dog laughs.
"I know that.
But I do.
And this is a good book.
See for yourself," he says.

Wolf takes the book.
It's big and heavy.
There's a dog on the cover.
The dog does not look like Dog.
Dog is white.
The dog on the book is black.
It's long-haired.
Its tongue hangs out.

"What a funny looking animal," says Wolf.
"A dog should be white.
A dog is white with a patch.
Like you, Dog."

Dog shakes his head.
"Not all dogs," he says.
"A dog can be white.
Or black. Or brown.
Or gray. Or brown with white.
Or black with brown.
Or brown with black.
It depends on the breed."
Wolf doesn't get it.
"What's a breed?" he asks.
"A breed is a type of dog," says Dog.
"Take a Boxer, for instance.
That's a type of dog.
Or a Pug.
Or a Bulldog.
A Boxer is a good watchdog.

A Bulldog is tough.
The Pug's nose is flat.
Each breed of dog has something special."

"You know so much!" says Wolf.
Dog smiles proudly.
He puffs out his chest.
"I've read a lot," he says.
"That's why.
I read my boss's book," Dog boasts.
"But now I've finished it.
You can have it for a while.
You're bound to learn something from it.
You might become as clever as me!"

Wolf growls.
He can't read a word.
Not one!
But he looks at the pictures.
He looks at every page.
There's so much to see!

He sees a breed of dog with long hair.
And a breed with short hair.
One breed has a curl in its tail.
Another has no tail at all!

Wolf looks for a breed that he knows.
He looks for Dog's breed.
But he can't find it.

"Dog, Dog!
What kind of breed are you?" asks Wolf.
Dog blushes.
"None," he says quietly.
"I'm half one thing, and half another."
"Oh," says Wolf.
He looks carefully at Dog.
He seems to be all in one piece.

"I don't have a family tree," Dog explains.
"Oh, is that all?" laughs Wolf.
"You can have one of my trees.
That oak there.

Or would you rather a beech?
A birch or a spruce?
Does the trunk have to be thick or thin?
Go ahead and choose.
I have a whole forest.
I won't miss one tree."
Dog sighs.
He shakes his head.
"A family tree isn't from the tree family, Wolf.
It doesn't grow in a forest.
A family tree is more like a leaf. A leaflet."

Wolf scratches his head.
"One little leaf of a tree?" he asks.
"First you wanted a trunk.
Now you want a leaf.
Next you'll be asking for a branch!
Or a treetop!
Or my whole forest!"

But Dog says:
"I don't mean a leaf from a tree.
A leaf is also a page in a book.
A leaflet is a page without a book.
On it is written the name of your father.
And the name of your mother.
And the name of your mother's father.
And the name of your mother's mother.
And the name of your father's…"
"Yes, yes, I get it," Wolf lies.
He's heard more than enough!

Dog claps the book shut.
He looks all around.
There's a tree, old and tall.
Dog grins.
"May I?" he asks.
He points at the tree.

Wolf grins as well.
He nods.
"It's not a family tree," says Dog.
"It's a tree trunk," says Wolf.
"Just the thing," says Dog.
He lifts his hind leg.
Wolf lifts his leg, too.
And they both water the tree.

HERO

Dog is sitting in his basket.
He looks out the window.
The boss isn't home.
Dog is keeping watch.
That's how it should be.

Now and then, Dog barks.
He barks at a bicycle on the road.
He barks at a leaf in the wind.
He barks at a cat by the gate.
That's his job.
It has to be done.
But it's so boring!

A man jogs by.
Dog barks.
A pigeon flies past.
Dog barks.
A mouse scampers through the grass.
Dog barks.

Dog yawns.
This is so, so boring!
If only there were a burglar!
If only a robber would come to the door!
Then you'd see some action.
Dog would bite the burglar's backside.
He'd be a hero!
Who knows, he might even be in the paper!

Dog yawns again.
He feels dopey and droopy.
Look, another bicycle.
Another leaf.
Another cat, another pigeon.

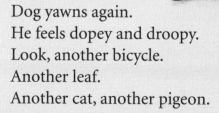

"Woof, woof," Dog barks feebly.
He's so tired!
Dog curls up in his basket.
"I won't fall asleep," he mutters.
"I'm keeping guard…for…my…"
Before you know it, Dog is quiet.
Next minute, he's snoring!

Dog dreams.
A bicycle flies past.
A man jogs along the hedge.
A cat blows in the wind.
And what's that in the grass?

Dog is scared.
It must be a burglar!
The burglar looks very savage.
He's waving a sharp knife.
Dog barks and barks.
But the burglar isn't scared.
He looks at Dog and grins.
And he taps at the window with the knife…

Dog whines and howls.
The burglar crawls in through the window.
Dog leaps from his basket.
"Help! Help!" he yelps.
"Boss, Boss, there's a burglar in the house!
Save me!"
He runs as fast as he can.
But the burglar runs after him.
He catches up with Dog!

"Dog! Dog!" the burglar calls.
"It's me, Wolf!"

What's happening?
The burglar's gone.
The knife's gone.
Dog is still in his basket.
And at the window is Wolf.

Wolf taps hard on the glass.
"At last!" Wolf growls.
"I thought you'd gone deaf."

"Dead?" Dog yelps.
He looks nervously at his coat.
Is there a hole in it?
Did the burglar stab him with the knife?
Is there any blood?
"I didn't say dead, I said deaf," says Wolf.
"Now let me in.
Quick!
Hurry up!"

Dog unlocks the door.
"About time," Wolf sighs.
He flops down on the couch.
His tongue hangs out.
He moans and groans.
"Oh, I feel so faint!
I was ringing the bell for over an hour.
Now I'm really hungry.
Famished, in fact!
Give me beer and meat and soup and cheese.
And half a dozen loaves of bread.
Heap the plate high.
I need to build up my strength!"

Dog does as Wolf says.
He fetches bread, soup, cheese, and porridge.
There's salami in the fridge.
He eats that himself.
Quickly, before Wolf sees it!

"Where's my beer?" Wolf grumbles.
"You're not having beer," says Dog firmly.

"All the beer belongs to my boss.
If you take it, you'll be a thief.
And I bite thieves…on the backside!"
Dog growls fiercely.

"Ha, ha!" Wolf roars with laughter.
"Dog, that's a joke!
You wouldn't bite.
You wouldn't dare.
You're much too meek."

Dog blushes.
He thinks of his dream.
He was so scared!
And it wasn't even real.

"I can be a hero if I need to," says Dog.
"I bark when I can, but I'll bite if I must.
Just you wait and see."

But no robber comes.
No burglar, either.
Only a cat and a pigeon.

And a man cycling down the street.
And the wind chasing a leaf.
Dog barks and barks.

And Wolf?
Wolf yawns and yawns.
This is so boring.
So very boring.
"What's keeping the robber?" he yawns.

Then:
"Is the burglar here yet?"

Dog is not amused.
"Go ahead and laugh, Wolf.
No burglar would dare to break in.
Thanks to the sign on the door.
It says:

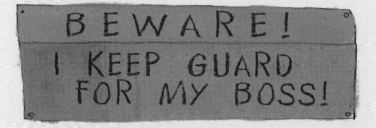

BEWARE!
I KEEP GUARD
FOR MY BOSS!

And that's what I do.
A burglar knows that.
The sign scares him off."

Wolf grins.
He says slowly:
"If you really are a hero…

Then you'll know how to deal with a kitty."

Now it's Dog's turn to laugh.
"A kitty!" he says.
"Are you a scaredy-cat, Wolf?"
"Oh, no," Wolf says quickly.
"I'm not scared.
What an idea.
But the kitty gets on my nerves.
She lives in my forest.
She acts as if it's hers.
And she won't leave."

"Bark at her," says Dog.
It's Wolf's turn to blush.
"I can't bark," he says.
"You know that, Dog.
I'm a wolf and I howl.
The kitty just laughs at me."

"Well, well," says Dog.
Wolf gives a big sigh.

He says:
"You have a good, loud bark.
Come on, Dog.
Come and bark for me.
Chase the kitty from the forest.
Then you'll be a true hero."

Dog doesn't think for long.
"I'll do it," he says bravely.
"But I want to be in the news."
"I'll see to it myself," says Wolf.
He spits on his claws.
He shakes Dog's paw.
"A wolf keeps his word," he says.
"Come as soon as the boss gets home."

"I will," says Dog. "Till then."
"Till then," says Wolf.

BARK

"So, here I am," says Dog.
"I'm here for the kitty.
You still want me?"
Wolf nods.
He looks at Dog.
Dog has a flask with him.
He takes a drink from it.

"What's in there?" asks Wolf.
Dog takes another swig.
He wipes his mouth.
"Strong stuff," he says.
"It soothes the throat.
I have to be in good voice.
No voice, no bark.
And it's all about the bark."
Dog screws the top back on the flask.
"Bring on the kitty, Wolf.
I'm ready for her!"

Wolf's forest is big.
There are no tracks.
But Wolf knows where to find the kitty.
Dog trots after him.
It's a long way.
Dog pants.

His tongue hangs out.
"Are we there yet?" he asks.
"It's such a long way and so hot!
I need a drink."
"Have another sip from your flask," says Wolf.
But Dog can't do that.
There's strong stuff in the flask.
One sip does no harm.
Two sips are fine.
But more than that?
Oh no.
That would make him sick.

"Here we are," Wolf says all at once.
He stops.

Wolf looks and Dog looks, too.
There's no kitty to be seen.

"Where is she?" Dog asks.
"There…or there." Wolf sounds vague.
"She'll turn up.
Now and then she goes off…
For an hour or so."

"An hour!" Dog yelps.
"I can't stay a whole hour!
What made you think I could?
I don't have time.
My basket waits for me."

"An hour's no time at all," says Wolf.
"The kitty might not come for a day.
Once she was gone a whole week.
I thought I was rid of her.
But I was wrong.
Out of the blue she came back.
To my forest!
As if it was hers.
There's one hill.
And on that hill stands one forest.
And I live in that forest.
There's no room for more."

Dog hears a "Hss!"
It comes from a tree.
"Hss, hss, hss!"

Something leaps to the ground.
What a beast!
So big!
So wild!
So fierce!

Dog gulps.
"That's not a kitty!" he yelps.
"That's a lion!"

Wolf laughs.
"Of course it isn't," he says.
"A lion doesn't hiss.

A lion roars.
A lion is big and yellow.
A lion has a mane.
No, Dog.
Have a good look.
This isn't a lion.
It really is a kitty!"

"I am not a kitty!
I'm a cat!" she spits at them.
"A kitty is small and soft.
A kitty sleeps in a lap.
A kitty eats meat from a can. But me?
I'm as wild as Wolf.
I'm a forest cat!
Hss!"

"A forest cat?
That's all very well.
But not in my forest!" cries Wolf.
He runs at the cat.
He snarls and howls.

And the cat?
She mocks him!
She hisses:
"*Sniff and snivel.*
Howl all day.
Crybaby, Wolf.
I won't go away!"

True, it rhymes.
But that doesn't mean Wolf likes it.
He shakes his fist.
The cat shows her claws.
"Scram, you brute!" Wolf yells.
"And watch out!
My cousin's here.
He'll bark you back up the tree."

The cat looks at Dog.
She gives a catty laugh.
"Is that your cousin, Wolf?
Did you think I'd be scared of that?
That shadow of a dog?"

"My cousin's a hero," says Wolf.
"You should hear him.
Go on, Dog.
Go on, bark!"

Dog coughs once.
He clears his throat.
"Weef!" is all he can manage.
Oh, great.
His bark has gone.
Thanks to the stress.
And there's nothing he can do about it.

The cat laughs.
"Now I've seen it all!
I had it wrong, Wolf.
Your cousin's not a dog.
Your cousin's a mouse!" she scoffs.
"But that suits me.
I have a taste for mice.
I'll eat him up, hide, hair, and all."
And she licks her lips…

Now Dog is angry, really angry!
"What? Me? A mouse?" he growls.
"How dare you!"
He swings his flask savagely about.

"There's a drink in here.
Strong stuff.
One swig makes me barking mad.
You watch and see."

What Dog says is not quite true,
The drink is to make his "weef" a "woof."

But the cat doesn't know this.
She turns pale.
She swallows.
She's not scared of a dog.
Nor of a wolf.
But a dog that's barking mad…
Dog unscrews the top of the flask.
He puts the flask to his mouth.
"Okay, okay," the cat says quickly.
"I was only joking."
She turns tail.
"I'll be on my way," she says.
"I've outstayed my welcome.
It was nice to see you, Wolf.
I'll call again sometime."
And she takes off.
Helter skelter!

Dog watches her go.
"What a beast," he growls.
"She called me a mouse.
That took some cheek!

Me, a dog!"
He takes a swig.
He burps.
"I'm a dog!" he says once more.

But Wolf says:
"Not only a dog, Dog.
You're a hero.
You got rid of the cat."

Dog takes another swig.
"Woof, woof!" he barks happily.

NEWSPAPER

Dog checks the mailbox.
Has the mail come yet?
It has!
There's the paper.
Dog skims it.
Is he in it?
Has Wolf kept his word?

No!

Dog turns each page.

He hunts and hunts.
He reads:

and

and

But it doesn't say:

Dog is furious.
He phones Wolf.

Wolf answers.
"Wolf," he says.
"Dog here!" Dog barks.
"Have you seen the paper yet?
If you have, you'll know how cross I am.
Very, very cross!
You said: '*A wolf keeps his word*.'
But that wasn't true.
You lied!
Because I'm not in the paper.
Even though I'm a hero.
You said so yourself."

Wolf laughs.
It's not a nice laugh.
"You're so stupid," he sniggers.
"I'm a wolf, so I lie.
You know that!
Okay, you're not in the paper.

So what?
Don't get in a knot over it.
Who reads the paper?
I don't!"

"But…"

"You chased off the cat.
That's what I wanted.
No more, no less.
The paper was bait.
And you took it!"

"You're such a liar!" Dog yelps.
Wolf laughs harder.
"Bye, Dog!
Nice of you to call.
But now I'm hanging up," he says.

"Beep, beep!" Dog hears.
Wolf has hung up.
Dog slams down the phone.

He is furious!
But there's nothing to be done.

Wolf sits in his forest.
He laughs himself silly.
How easy it was to trick Dog.
He isn't a bit sorry.
Oh, no!
A wolf is still a wolf.
He bites when he's hungry.
He lies when it suits him.
Bad luck for Dog.
But Wolf's tickled pink!

Dog lies in his basket.
He plans to wreak his revenge.

Wreak is a strange word.
You see a *w*,
but you hear an *r*.
So it should really be:
reak his revenge.

"I'll get Wolf back," growls Dog.
"I'll be as wily as he is.
It'll do me good.
Because revenge is sweet!"
Dog thinks and thinks.
And all at once he knows!
He has a plan.
A really cunning plan…

Wolf is in his forest.
He whistles a tune.
But what's this?
Here comes a kitty!
This kitty is soft and white.
She waves a paper.
"Hello!" she calls out.

"Are you Wolf?"
Wolf gasps.
What is this kitty doing here?
What does she want from him?
The kitty walks straight up to Wolf.
She stands right in front of his nose!

"What are you after?" growls Wolf.
"Are you Wolf?" the kitty asks again.
"What's that to you?" Wolf snarls.
"I've come about the forest," she says.
"The forest?" asks Wolf.
"Yes," nods the kitty.
"The forest mentioned in the paper.
I saw it in the TO RENT column."

The kitty shows Wolf the paper.
This is what it says:

Wolf blushes.
He can't read a word.
He doesn't know how.
He can't tell an *a* from a *b*.
"Read it to me.
I don't have my glasses," he fibs.

"Okay," says the kitty.
She reads:
"Big forest available.
Good for kitties.
Cats also allowed.
Ask for Wolf."
Then she folds up the paper.
"Is the forest still available?" she asks.

"Or am I too late?"

"Too late?" shrieks Wolf.

"Too late?

You're far too early!

This is my forest and it's not available.

Go away because I'm very angry!

I don't want to see you here ever again!"

The kitty arches her back.

Her tail fluffs out.

"Hss! You're so scary!" she hisses.

"Very, very scary!" snarls Wolf.

"What did you expect?

I'm wild!

I'm a wolf!

I'll bite you!

I'll savage you!"

Wolf snaps his teeth at the kitty.

But she's fast.

Much too fast for Wolf!

"Here, take this!" she yowls.

And she hits Wolf.
With the paper! On his head!
Then she scrams.

Wolf rubs his head.
He's furious.
His forest is not for rent.
And yet it said so in the paper.
How can that be?
Who did it?
"Dog," says Wolf.
"I bet Dog knows something about this."

Wolf phones Dog.
Dog answers.
"Dog here," says Dog.

"Who's this?
And what can I do for you?"
"A whole lot!" Wolf rages.
"I'm angry, very angry!"
"Oh?" says Dog.

"Yes. You played a nasty trick.
Admit it.
You wrote that my forest was for rent.
You set a cat on me.
How dare you!" Wolf yells.

But Dog laughs.
"Did you like that, Wolf?
Or can't you take a joke?"
Now Wolf is really wild.
"A joke? Call that a joke?
My forest was in the paper!"

Dog stops laughing.
"Ah, Wolf," he says.
"There's no need to get so worked up.
Who reads the paper anymore?"

"But…"

"Bye, Wolf!
It was nice of you to call.

But now I'm going to hang up."

"Beep, beep," Wolf hears.
Dog has hung up.
Wolf slams down the phone.
Boy, is he wild!
Dog has outwitted him.

And he can't do a thing about it!
Rats!

THIEF

It's nighttime.
Dog is asleep.
The boss is asleep.
There's no moon.
All the lights are off.
There's not a star in the sky.
The night is as dark as ink.
And a thief is prowling round the house.

Does Dog see the thief?
No.
Does he hear anything?
No!
The thief is very quiet.
Dog is sleeping.
His basket is soft and warm.
He's having a lovely dream.

The thief is at the door.
His coat is big and black.

He has a stocking on his head.
You can't see who he is.
The thief doesn't knock.
He doesn't ring the bell.
But he doesn't break in either.
What does the thief want?
What's he doing now?
No!
He's stealing the sign from the door!
The sign with:

BEWARE!
I KEEP GUARD FOR MY BOSS!

The thief stuffs the sign into a sack.
He takes a good look around.
Then he creeps quietly away.

It's daytime.
Dog yawns.
The sun's already up.
But the boss isn't.
Dog leaves his basket.
He heads for the garden.
He lifts his leg.
Ah, that's better!
Only then does he see the sign.
Or rather, he doesn't see it.
Because the sign is gone.
What a calamity!

"Boss! Boss!
Come quickly!
There's been a thief!" Dog barks.
"A thief who's stolen the sign!"
But the boss doesn't come.
He's still in bed.
He doesn't want to get up.

"Too bad," growls Dog.
"I'll sort it out myself, then.
I know what to do.
I'm not a hero for nothing!"

First Dog sniffs at the door.
"Hmm," he says.
Then he presses his nose to the grass.

He takes a deep sniff.
Once. Twice.
A third time.
Is he on the thief's trail?
"Hmm…" says Dog again.

He scratches his head.
"How strange," he says.
"I don't smell a thief.
I smell…I smell…
I smell Wolf!"

All at once Dog works it out.
"I know what!" he cries.
"Wolf is the thief!"

Could that be true?
It could!
Once a wolf, always a wolf.
He bites when he's hungry.
He lies when it suits him.
He steals whatever he wants.
Wolf is as wild as wild can be.

Now Dog is wild with Wolf.
He hurries from the garden.
He doesn't need to follow the scent.

He knows the way!
He runs straight to the forest.

And look!
Dog sees the sign up ahead.
A coat lies beside it.
And a stocking.

Dog sniffs the coat and the stocking.
"Just as I thought," he growls.
"A strong whiff of Wolf.
He's the thief.
No doubt about it.
I've got him now.
The sparks are going to fly!"

Wolf has just sat down to his meal.
His mouth is stuffed full.
Fat drips down his chin.
He guzzles and gobbles and gulps.
"Ah, Dog!" Wolf smacks his lips.
"How nice of you to come!"

"There's nothing nice about it," Dog growls.
"I've come for my sign."
Wolf grins.
"Your sign? Which sign?
I don't have a sign.
I have a pan.
As you can see, I eat straight from it.
There's room in the pan for more.
I'm going to fill it up.

Come and sit down at my pan.
I like to share food when I can."

Wolf laughs.
"That rhymes!" he says.
"I just love rhyme.
Rhyme's sublime.
But what I said is true as well.
I'm not a mean Wolf.
There's plenty here for you, Dog.
Come and eat with me."
Wolf tosses Dog a bone.

"Would you like that?
Or a slice of ham?
Or a slab of steak, cooked rare?
A chunk of sausage or a chicken leg?
Oh, dear!

I know.
You don't want any. You're too plump already.
As round as a log is Dog!"

Wolf roars with laughter.
Dog can't see the funny side.
"You stole my sign, Wolf," he says.
"You're a thief.
A stupid one at that.
Because it says on the sign:

BEWARE!
I KEEP GUARD FOR MY BOSS!

What do you want with that thing?
You don't even have a boss.
Who are you keeping guard for?"

Wolf's fun is over.
He looks down at his paws.
"I keep guard of my forest.
That's close enough," he says.
"Ha, ha!" Dog scoffs.

"A forest is not a boss," he says.
"Who cares," says Wolf.
"As long as the sign helps.
It scares off the cats and the kitties as well.
That's what counts."
"But the sign is *mine*," says Dog.
"And the forest is *mine*," says Wolf.
"What can I do about that?"

Dog and Wolf are quiet for a while.

"I know what," Dog says suddenly.
"I'll make a new sign.
A sign for you, Wolf!
I know that you're wild.
You bite and lie and steal.
You burp.
You never blow your nose.
You don't read the paper.
But you're my cousin.
And once a cousin, always a cousin.
So I'll help you.
That's only fair."

"Really?" Wolf asks happily.
"Do something for me then.
Make me a sign that says:

I ROREST FOR MY FOREST!"

"Don't be silly!" Dog laughs.
"There's no such word as ROREST!"

"But it rhymes.
And I want my sign to rhyme," Wolf insists.
Dog gives it some thought.
"Okay," he says.
"Your sign will rhyme.
I'll make sure of it."
"Shake on it?"
"Shake on it," says Dog.
He spits on his paw.

Wolf spits on his.
"A dog keeps his word," says Dog.
Then he goes home.
But he takes his sign with him.
Wolf is going to get his own sign.
A sign that rhymes!

"Is my sign ready yet, Dog?"
"No. The paint's still wet."
"May I see it?"
"It's in the shed."
"Where?"
"There, in the corner."

I tremble in fear
of my cousin dear

"What does it say?"
"Does that matter?
You can't read it anyway."
"But does it rhyme?"
"Yes."
"That's okay then."

First American edition published in 2013 by Gecko Press USA,
an imprint of Gecko Press Ltd.

Distributed in the United States and Canada by
Lerner Publishing Group, Inc.
241 First Avenue North
Minneapolis, MN 55401 USA
www.lernerbooks.com

A catalog record for this book is available from the
US Library of Congress.

This edition first published in 2013 by Gecko Press
PO Box 9335, Marion Square, Wellington 6141, New Zealand
info@geckopress.com

© 2009, Uitgeverij Lannoo nv. For the original edition.
Original title: Wolf en Hond. Translated from the Dutch language.
www.lannoo.com

English language edition © Gecko Press Ltd 2013
Translation © Bill Nagelkerke 2013

Edited by Penelope Todd
Typeset by Vida & Luke Kelly Design, New Zealand
Printed by Everbest, China

ISBN hardback (USA): 978-1-877579-47-9
ISBN paperback: 978-1-877579-38-7

For more curiously good books,
visit www.geckopress.com

This book was published with the support of the
Dutch Foundation for Literature and the Flemish
Literature Fund (www.flemishliterature.be)

Nederlands
letterenfonds
dutch foundation
for literature

Flemish
Literature
Fund